LIZ GARTON SCANLON
and AUDREY VERNICK

illustrated by
OLIVIER TALLEC

FIVE
MINUTES

(That's a lot of time) (No, it's not) (Yes, it is)

G. P. PUTNAM'S SONS

For Barbara. This just took five minutes! —L.G.S.

For the generous Adria Glass, with thanks for the brilliant idea. —A.V.

G. P. PUTNAM'S SONS

an imprint of Penguin Random House LLC, New York

Visit us online at penguinrandomhouse.com

Library of Congress Cataloging–in–Publication Data

Names: Scanlon, Elizabeth Garton, author. | Vernick, Audrey, author. | Tallec, Olivier, illustrator.

Title: Five minutes (that's a lot of time) (no, it's not) (yes, it is) / by Liz Garton Scanlon and Audrey Vernick; illustrated by Olivier Tallec.

Description: New York, NY: G. P. Putnam's Sons, [2019]

Summary: Throughout a child's day, five minutes can go by quickly (when you are on a roller coaster) or slowly (when you are in the dentist's chair).

Identifiers: LCCN 2018031344 | ISBN 9780525516316 (hc) | ISBN 9780525516323 (epub fxl cpb) | ISBN 9780525516347 (kf8/kindle)

Subjects: | CYAC: Time—Fiction.

Classification: LCC PZ7.S2798 Fi 2019 | DDC [E]—dc23

LC record available at https://lccn.loc.gov/2018031344

Manufactured in China by RR Donnelley Asia Printing Solutions Ltd.

ISBN 9780525516316

10 9 8 7 6 5 4 3 2 1

Design by Eileen Savage and Suki Boynton. Text set in Memo STD.

The art was done in pencil and acrylic paint.

Five minutes is a lot of time.

Wait—no, it's not!

Five minutes is forever!

Five minutes is an eternity!

Only five
minutes?

Five minutes is too long.

Five minutes is way too long.

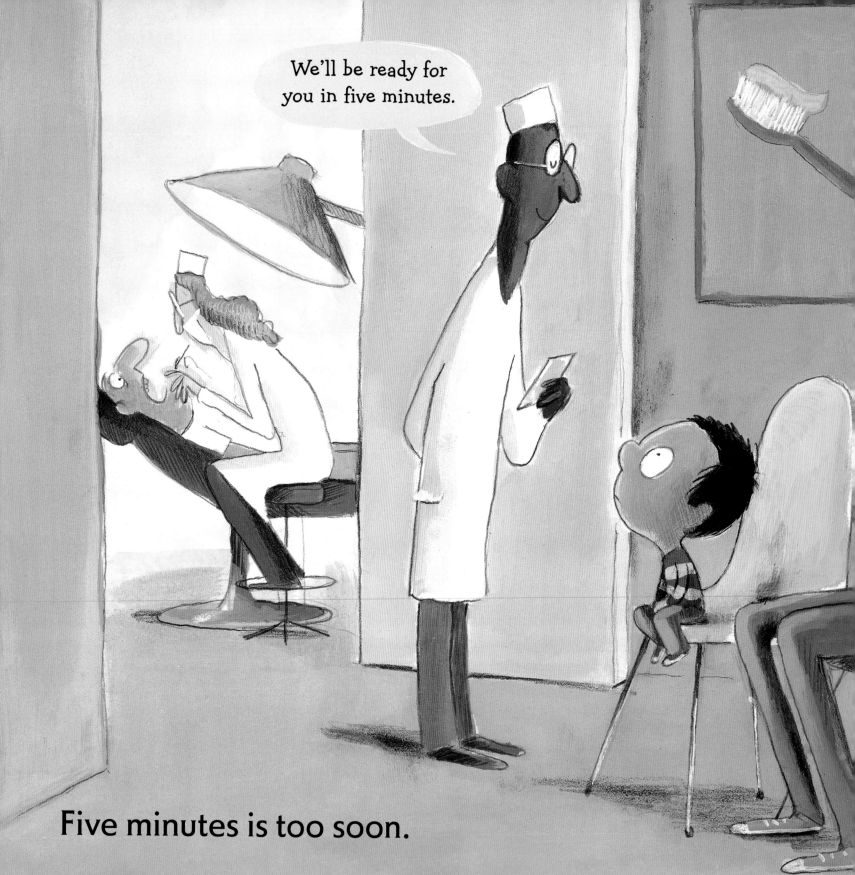

Five minutes is too soon.

Five minutes is not soon enough.

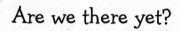

How am I supposed to wait five minutes?

Finally!

Five minutes is five minutes is five minutes.

Five minutes is a lifetime!

Aw, man. Five minutes flies by!

Sometimes.

Please? Just five more minutes?

Seriously. Hang on.

It's already been five minutes?

Five minutes is endless!

Five minutes is a waste of five minutes.

Five minutes is not enough minutes.

Even five *extra* minutes is not enough minutes.

Except for sometimes,
when five minutes is just right.

(Especially when it's
actually ten minutes.)